YOUR BODY IS A HOUSE STRIPPED

Charley Barnes is a Lecturer in Creative and Professional Writing. She specialises in crime fiction, and has authored several novels in this genre, too, though her preferred style is psychological thrillers. Now, Charley is writing her first academic monograph, forthcoming with Palgrave Macmillan, while also working on her twelfth novel. She continues to collaborate with other poets, namely Claire Walker and Wendy Allen, and she is readying her second full manuscript of poetry to step out into the world.

Also by Charley Barnes

Books marked with * are published under Charlotte Barnes

Your Body is a House Stripped

Charley Barnes

Broken Sleep Books

ISBN: 978-1-915760-15-9

Cover designed by Aaron Kent

Edited & Typeset by Aaron Kent

Broken Sleep Books Ltd
Rhydwen
Talgarreg
Ceredigion
SA44 4HB

Broken Sleep Books Ltd
Fair View
St Georges Road
Cornwall
PL26 7YH

Contents

Weight

Wait

There is no better kept secret than the thing everyone knows, but no one is willing to talk about.

Weight

One

Imagine this:

Your body is a house stripped from the pages of a Gothic novel. There was a fire once, in the hearth of the home, and it burned through the soft furnishings. It took with it the comfort of crushed velvet curtains and the grand armchairs you once enjoyed quiet afternoons in. The books – oh, the books you lost: *Great Expectations*, *Persuasion*, *As I Lay Dying*. The shelves bowed against the heat and were buried under the weight of hot paperbacks and hard covers. Your body – the house, that is – became an origami structure where one room folded or fell neatly into another. Things that were once upstairs now sat in the belly of the building. The skylight was no longer a panel but the whole head of your structure; fragmented and gaping with crisp white remains around the edges. Cracks between blown-out windows and their frames whistled with every wind that ran through you, and for a long time that was the only noise.

The authorities investigated what had caused the fire, citing several points of origin. The kitchen seemed the most likely space – with the wide-open mouths of angry pots and the fury of the stove. There was always something to be cut and cooked and force-fed, and it wouldn't surprise you if the constant stream of steaming foods had led to this structural collapse – it was a theory you kept to yourself even though others mentioned it, too. Although, of course, there were those who accused *you* of being the cause – as though you'd do such a thing, and to your own ~~body~~ home.

Two

Getting dressed in the morning isn't as easy as it used to be. Partly because you can't stand to look at your body in the mirror and partly because you can't not look at your body in the mirror. You make your ribs into a tally chart of days since you've done things: enjoyed a snack; eaten with your family; liked yourself. You can't get dressed quickly enough in clothes that are too big for you, but in being too big they hide that you're ~~too small~~ not small enough. It used to be an idle pleasure, seeing yourself smaller in things that used to be just right. Goldilocks was the first to teach us that finding things that are just right for ourselves can often lead to some kind of catastrophe though. So with that in mind maybe it's no wonder that you're trying something too small. *You tried too big already*. You shake that thought away – the intrusive one that speaks in your hard voice but not with a soft tongue – all the while thinking how right it is. You finish preparing yourself for the day by painting on a face that feels clown-like but everyone loves that you're wearing more make-up now. They call it "experimenting with your style" but it feels more like hiding in plain sight.

When you leave the bathroom, fully clothed and desperate for a cup of tea, you collide with your mother in the hallway.

'Those clothes are getting too big for you,' she says.

'Oh, shush, they are not.'

'They are, love, I can see a real difference.'

This hurts you. You've never kept anything from her, not really. You may have hidden the occasional crafty smoke when you were younger, or the odd night out on the lash when you were "staying at a mate's and going straight to college". But everyone was hiding those sorts of things. The girls – when you were all young enough for it to be trendy – they tried to hide their eating disorders, too. In the same way that you grew out of your puppy fat, they grew out of their brittle bones and into their beautiful bodies. You did it the wrong way around, though, like a body-myth that shows the protagonist becoming thinner – weaker, more angular – as the story progresses. It feels like a regression when you think of it this way – as though a mental illness is something you're allowed when you're younger, but by the time you're pushing thirty you should know better.

'These clothes are as old as the hills, Mum, they're just stretched out.'

'Well, we should get you some new ones then.'

'But these are comfortable.' She'll have an answer for this – there's one for everything – so you try to cut the chord of one conversation in favour of another. 'Do you want a brew, anyway? I'm desperate for a drink.'

'Yeah, will you bring it up?'

'Course.'

You love the quiet of the morning downstairs. For a while you don't have to think about anything but the task at hand, which is usually answering emails, and taking phone calls. You're working remotely now – it's a brave new world, mid-pandemic – which means you don't have to contend with colleagues either. You handle several social media accounts for a small advertising company, although you're one of many helping hands at the job, so the company hasn't really felt small for a while. There's enough to keep you all busy and out of each other's ways, bar the occasional instant message to ask something that isn't usually related to work.

While the kettle boils you lean back against the kitchen counter. You pretend not to notice how uncomfortable the work surface is against the braille of your spine. The garden looks beautiful. You've put a lot of effort into scattering seeds liberally about the place and hoping for the best, and it seems to have really paid off. There are small wild gardens appearing in clusters, as though each set of seeds has formed a faction, and you wonder whether they're planning to overthrow the sunflowers.

There's so much food on the work surface. It's nothing offensive or drastic; nothing that you wouldn't eat – if you could stand to. There's a glass biscuit jar packed full of custard creams, hobnobs, rich tea, digestives. Smaller jars have smaller sweets; chocolate buttons, ice gems, raisins, peanuts. Your mum hasn't had a sit-down conversation with you about food, but oh, she's talking about it. You eye each container up and down like a suspect in a criminal case and you consider trying to convince yourself to eat something. But it's only mid-morning and you know you can do better than this.

When the kettle's boil whistles to a close you make the drinks and treat this as a distractor task. You're aware eating is important – you understand how the human body works, that is – but there are lots of other important things in the world that also aren't being done. On days like today that feels like a justification for leaving your stomach empty. Although you've arrived at a point in your "recovery" where you no longer know whether you want to feel empty, or full – nor do you know whether these words have anything to do with food.

You take hardly any milk in your tea; your mum takes a lot in hers. On your way back through the kitchen towards the stairs, you leave your own cuppa on the desk to wait, to cool. You can hear the chattering of a phone call overhead – your mum and one of the many insurance companies she's having to contend with mid-pandemic – and you hope this means she won't ask *the* question. And yet–

'Have you eaten something?' She covers the speaker to ask.

You bite back an eye roll. 'I'll have a cereal bar when I go downstairs.' You won't. You'll unwrap a cereal bar, cover it carefully in swathes of tissue and bury it at the bottom of the bin. Then you'll strategically leave the wrapper on the top of the rubbish pile, making sure that it's an unavoidable eye-catcher for whoever uses the bin next. This is how you ~~don't~~ eat breakfast now.

'Tea break later?'

'Sure, I've got an important call for work in around ten minutes, then a meeting.'

She understands your meaning. 'Yes, I'll be quiet.'

'Thanks, Mum.'

'Love you, kid.'

'You too.'

She's worried sick about you. There's a conversation to be had that neither of you are willing to initiate yet – it'll come, you're sure. But even without speaking you can see small changes in her look; the way her eyebrows pull together in a near-constant frown. When she hugs you now, you can't help but feel as though she's sizing you up. You've become Gretel, too skinny to do anything of use with and so everyone around you tries to feed you, without telling you the real reason for why. Sometimes you fantasise about them putting you in a mixing pot and boiling you down to nothing. It's when you think about things like that you realise food isn't about food at all; it's about magic. You'd like to make yourself the disappearing woman/man. Like those famous illusionists who make their bodies origami, corners and edges tight enough to stash into a box. But when your curtain is lifted you'd like to not be there at all.

Your tea is cool enough to drink by the time you're at your desk. You've got a good six minutes before the phone starts ringing so you take in greedy mouthfuls (oh, greed, now you're The Ungrateful Son, and you wonder whether the Grimms might put a forever-frog on your face to stop you from ~~not~~ eating). The fairytale references are many in your head. You spent a significant portion of your life studying them – a waste of a degree if ever there was one, your sibling ~~says~~ jokes – but they help you to see things differently. Your counsellor calls it transference. You call it getting through the day.

By the time the phone rings you're two thirds of the way through your cup of tea and you're glad because you always forget to drink during these conversations – sometimes breathe, too, but that's down to the crying. Your counsellor says it will get easier. But they're bound to say that, aren't they?

Three

Imagine this:

Your body is a terrace house in a nice area. Let's call the area: Gender Expectations. Gender Expectations has a long-standing reputation in the wider community of the world, and the reputation needs to be upheld by everyone who lives in the area. Because of that, the front of your terrace is sometimes criticised by others for not quite being in-keeping with the aesthetic of the street. These others – the ones with neat front gardens and walls painted in appropriate colours – will advise you on how to make your front-facing exterior more suitable. A good start, they tell you, is to pick either pink or blue flowers, and adorn your land with them as clearly as possible. It isn't entirely inappropriate to plant yellow, but these flowers should be limited to a select few, rather than being something that might dominate the landscape. Once these flowers are planted and in full bloom, passers-by will get a better sense of who your house is as a person. You also have the option of painting the house itself. Either side of you there are blue/pink houses in varying shades of pastel through to neon. The others, they tell you that you can choose whatever gradient you like, and they look at you with some suspicion when you ask for something like beige – or even a pale butter, custard. But you all agree beige would be for the best.

Neighbours ask you how many rooms your house has. What they really mean to ask is whether there's space for a human within you, human; can you make your body a home? You consider asking them why you'd let someone else live in this space. Why, when you struggle to find the heart of the home, why, when you struggle to love the papered walls and the exposed beams, why, you would erect another house on a street full of demolition workers.

You huff and puff and blow your own house down. You leave behind blue bricks and pink rafters. They all wonder why you were so desperate to move out.

Four

You re-hydrated before bed which means you're heavier this morning than you want to be which means you've let yourself down – again. You haven't, not really. But you pin that self-compassion to the wall and fling darts at it in the hours that follow your weigh-in. To help matters, when you go downstairs your step-parent eyes you up and down like a slab of meat on the turn.

They say, 'That bra/t-shirt/body is too small for you.'

And your heartbeat becomes a thunder drum that shakes your rib cage. You laugh along with them even though nothing they've said is funny, and they should know better, and your actual parent should have warned them about triggers – and the list of reasons why you shouldn't be laughing stretches on and on, reeling itself out behind you as you rush for the stairs. When you're in the bathroom alone that's when the panic really starts. The attack comes too quickly and you wonder whether this, too, is a way to burn calories. Although if that were true then you would have disappeared by now, or at the very least, become small enough.

With each chest heave you count a calorie still; with every tear you think of the dehydration, how much less your body will weigh without that water. Your reflection copies these beats of panic and you watch as you both spiral into something too dark for this early in the day – when there's a whole late morning, afternoon, evening left to get through.

Your actual parent taps the door, then, and asks, 'Are you okay?'

You borrow a normal person's steady tone for long enough to say, 'Yes, thank you.'

'Can you come to see me before you go downstairs?'

And you assume this is for an apology by proxy.

'Sure thing.'

But it isn't.

Instead your parent says, 'Don't pay any attention.'

You wonder where this advice was when you were a child and

diet culture was shoved down your tight throat like fresh kale. You wonder where *don't pay any attention* was when you were bigger than you are now, and you asked if you could diet because people didn't like you as you were. *Don't pay attention* to numbers in and around your body, populating the planet as much as subatomic particles do. *Don't pay attention—*

'Did you hear what I said?'

'Don't pay attention?'

'They don't mean anything by it.'

'No,' you say, 'no, I know. It's okay.'

These things have never been okay but you're a master of making them seem as though they are. From a child you've been taught how to use make-up to make-up everything not-okay into okay-enough which is both part of the problem and part of the fix.

'Have you eaten?' your parent asks.

'Yes,' you say, even though you haven't and can't bring yourself to. 'Biscuit with my tea.' You've learnt how to provide just enough of the lie for it to sound like a truth, and even though your parent eyes you suspiciously they don't push the issue further because why would anyone lie about *one* biscuit? It's hardly a detail worth embellishing but you know, still, that these are key details now. You leave them like breadcrumbs in your wake and the people who are trying to make sure you don't die gobble them freely in a way that you're envious of. You pick the breadcrumbs that are best for you, with the best numbers – because it comes down to the numbers, always – and you sprinkle them, setting one carefully in front of your parent before backing away slowly while they eat. You place them out an equal distance from each other – 'Yes, a few peanuts.' – tracking them down the stairs, every few steps – 'I'll have a piece of toast later.' – and then a small cluster at the base of the decline – 'I'm really looking forward to ~~eating whatever it is you want me to eat~~ takeaway night because I've been fancying pizza all week, might even go large.' – because they'll chew on that for hours.

You place the breadcrumbs strategically throughout the day – 'I had half a sandwich while I was in town.' – leaving clusters in different rooms of the house, unspoken sometimes – an empty wrapper for a chocolate bar you ~~didn't eat~~ ate – because it's too obvious to spell everything out overtly. The clues are there, though, and by the time they're dishing up your dinner plate – 'Just a small portion, please.' – you've left enough red herrings about the place to justify not having an extra roast potato/piece of bread/anything, because

'I've been eating

on and off

the whole day

long, and really

I'm so full

~~of bad feeling~~

that I hardly have room

for anything ~~good~~ at all.'

Five

Imagine this:

Your body is a woodland cottage, tumbled from the pages of a book that was read to you when you were younger. The structure is the same as it's always been, made up of two-hundred and six small splinters of wood that hold you together in a way that appears habitable but you are looking for ways to ~~move out~~ downsize. There are parts of the cottage that are in a state of disrepair and you've been taught from a young age not to live with superficial imperfections. The walls have dampened from intermittent ~~tears~~ rain, though, and the wooden beams are bowing like the floor is royalty. This structural sag is one of many issues that means the skin of the place doesn't fit how it used to. Although you realise that becoming smaller than a cottage on the outskirts of the woods will be a challenge even for you, but you are nothing if not self-disciplined about your ~~body~~ home.

There are times, though, when you find yourself in the pages of those childhood books still. You believe that you were beautiful – then. A long time ago, back down the tracks of a winding narrative that predates the villagers and their burning torches.

Sometimes, to make your ~~readers~~ relatives and friends happy, you'll leave breadcrumbs on the outskirts of your property even now. They will be full and home-baked and spongy on the tongue, so people are happy to consume them. But when they run short they come looking for you – for more of the un-truths you've told them, and you become the villain of your own story because *you're* the one that's been lying. When they arrive on your doorstep, with their hands cupped as though they're Oliver's friends, begging please, for more of these palatable things, they will realise the rot of the place. And they will back away from the stench and moss of the outer walls with their noses pegged, telling you all the while that it's okay because you're a beautiful person – on the inside.

Six

Now, it isn't only your body that takes up too much space. Your thoughts about your body also take up too much space. Like Alice, you had too much cake or wine – both, knowing you – and now you're shrinking and expanding compulsively so your thoughts are spilling out of windows, through the front door, flooding the garden so even the neighbours are stopping to ask, 'Is s/he okay?'

Your parent(s) say: 'Yes, just back home again.'

They've asked you to talk, but they did so under the misapprehension that it would be one conversation – two, at a push. That it would be a few weeks of difficult eating but that once you'd broken the back of the problem then you'd be able to power through, an army of small soldiers clearing away the debris of battle. But there's an unexpected dragon/ogre/witch/wolf/mother who leaves another breadcrumb trail – not unlike your own, except this one is for you and not your family. You greedily gobble down ideas about your lack of self-awareness and control; how you don't have any discipline; how you're a weak person for *letting this happen*. You eat so many breadcrumbs that eventually they pour forth from your open mouth like you're a fountain of self-aimed insults and everyone around you says, 'But you were getting better.' and, 'You've been doing well.'

For fear of letting them down, again, you swallow the breadcrumbs instead, until you're the size of a house. But wait, your inner narrative adds, weren't you already the size of a house? Two houses, then, a whole street!

'You're quiet,' your Mum says, and you're glad of the interruption. 'Work. I've got lots on.'

You recycle the lie, 'I'm better when I've got lots on.' You have said this so many times now that you believe it to be absolute truth, like death and sugar taxes. In place of food, you fill your days with projects and bright ideas and other things that spark a fire behind your eyes, fierce enough for you to warm yourself and those around you, even though you've been cold for weeks. That happens, you know, and you take it to be good ~~bad~~ sign that you must be doing well ~~getting worse~~. There are times when you will share these blazing schemes with loved ones and your parent might say, 'Are you sure you aren't taking too much on?' But your worth is inextricably bound to this much-ness, this on-ness and besides, 'It's all fun, though, isn't it?' you can answer, knowing that you aren't lying. You are telling so many lies now that the truth feels cucumber in ice water refreshing.

Though the real truth isn't something you can share, of course. Because the real truth is that you pride yourself on being so busy, so buried, that the wall clock will take its hands, gather up the arbitrary minutes of the day attributed to mealtimes, and deposit them into your working hours instead. It is easy to forget to eat.

'Are you stopping for dinner?'

'I'm not really hungry.'

'What have you had today?'

Nothing, you have had nothing. 'I've been snacking all day while I've been working. I dread to think how much I've eaten.' You probably don't even look up from the keyboard of your laptop as you say this. You may have even staged the scene with a wrinkled wrapper from a breakfast bar – here's one I saved earlier, before burrowing the tightened oats to the base of the bin – and a Pringles tub. 'I wouldn't mind a drink, if you're making one?' You have read online that caffeine can be an appetite suppressant but you're no longer convinced your appetite exists.

'Stop soon, won't you?' your Mum asks. There is a flicker of worry somewhere behind the words that makes shadow puppets of them on a nearby wall and you remember, then, the shapes she used to make when telling you a bedtime story about a thin princess who was wanted by *all* of the boys and sometimes even the dragons.

'Stop worrying, won't you?' you say in a jovial tone.

She ruffles your hair. 'It's my job to.'

'Worry about me dehydrating,' you say and nudge your empty mug towards her. You wink and continue typing. She gives in and flicks the kettle to boil. She tells you about her day and the worrying stops and you wonder whether you *are* dehydrated – it is a strange hope to have. But you think of the garden flowers and how they wilt without water; how when there is so little water and enough heat applied, too, they will shrink.

But when you step on the scales the following morning you find that your weight is lower, again, and suddenly the dry mouth and the lips like old pavement don't seem like such a huge sacrifice to have made. You tell your counsellor this, how the weight decrease feels like an achievement, still. They ask whether you could try to reframe that narrative, to read: Weight maintenance is an achievement. They suggest, too, that you might not have to try drinking more but drinking earlier. Eating earlier. You nod and agree because in principle this makes sense. In practice, it makes sense. It is advice that you would give to a loved one. You would squeeze their hand, rub the back of it, even, gently though so not to hurt the bones that bulge like cartoon outlines. You would speak to the loved one softly and say that there is nothing inherently wrong with drinking or eating or with weight gain. You tell your counsellor that you would do this, you underscore, <u>for a loved one</u>.

You say nothing to them about not loving yourself. This is a conversation you can't stand to have again. Instead, you cry for a while after the session and wonder whether this, too, is a method for dehydrating. So you sob, and you sob, and then you find a patch of sun because it is the only way you can feel warm now, and you wilt there. And you hope that people ~~will won't will won't~~ notice the weight loss.

Seven

Imagine this:

Your body is a green house. The structure is unremarkable, though it has served its purpose for years. It is what's inside that counts, people tell you. For some time, inside has in fact been empty; you have cultivated it that way. What little soil there was went underwatered to the extent that growth – real and beautiful growth, the type that people can appreciate in an Instagram reel[1] – became impossible. You coveted this hollow interior in the hope that one day lookers might be able to see right through.

Though you did not realise that this, too, was a kind of growth. You had overlooked the weeds – the ones that appear in city-wide slabs of foundation – and the self-seeding wildflowers that arrive without a welcome invite. So soon, things *were* growing, and you were encouraged by professionals to appreciate the mess and knots of stems overlapped; the way pollen would weep onto the floor when someone paid you a compliment. Fruit began to bloom, too, and you would often be found, sphere in hand and juice running down chin, feasting on your own harvest. People commented on these observable changes; applauses that you were a Venus flytrap for. Your plant pots were soon so overflowing with joy and colour, that no one noticed when you wrapped your fingers around the body of a sunflower and yanked it right free with its root, or when you forgot to water vegetable beds. You soon made it a challenge, to see

---

1.   You admire the aesthetic of 'What I eat in a day' videos but the reality is that they only compound your dislike of yourself and your love of your sickness. These videos are often made by people already smaller than you, which leads you to believe that rather than implementing extensions on the property of your body, it can only be right that you must knock it down further, so that one day you might be able to build it back together using yogurt, fresh fruit, and a filter that looks especially good on a square grid. Later reflection will help you to see that this social media friendly recovery is not the recovery you aspire to, because none of the 3,000 strangers who read your current posts actually give a shit about whether you die from a mental illness.

what you could kill off without anyone noticing. If you were careful enough, you thought you might manage to bulldoze your body back down.

Eight

You need to be seen to be relaxing. This, as much as everything else you do, is a show now. Your prop is a cup of tea that you feel guilty for drinking; overlaid, like a revised blueprint, on top of the guilt you feel for having had breakfast because this, too, is something that needs to be seen during these times when people are testing your ability to function. You imagine yourself test tube small and held up to a strip of light, a parent flicking at the base of you, watching how things simmer and mix and react. You react with faux calm when someone offers you fruit even though you have had this breakfast and a fudge-covered pretzel. You wonder how your puppet nose will withstand this spinning wheel of lies you tell, now, whether your nose, too, will expand and lengthen and knock sweet jars from their shelves in the kitchen.

An additional prop in this pantomime you have created is a book. It is a throwaway ten-a-penny detective novel with a nondescript cover and an interesting enough plot that it might hold your attention long enough to read through lunch and into dinner. You need something good enough to help you to forget a meal; this is your barometer for quality.

By page fifty-eight you have started to pencil underline all of the comments regarding a woman's weight in the book: 'She doesn't want to play the damsel in distress again. It's not a flattering look for an X-stone woman.'[2]

'You're underlining loads,' your parent comments. 'Is it a good one?'

They're not especially interested in your answer. They're trying to make conversation, though, and you appreciate the effort. Though you also appreciate that what is about to happen – if you answer

---

2.   Of course, this remains censored because you are not foolish enough to isolate a single bracket of woman to throw shame on. It is not your place to care how heavy other people are. You only care about how small they appear, and X-stone tells you nothing of a person's size, only their relationship to gravity.

honestly, that is – is that you will take a strong steel implement and use it to score around the edge of a brim-full can of worms. They will spill out onto the floor and echo things like, 'Aren't you reading too much into this?' and, 'I'm sure the author didn't do it to actually be offensive.' These echoes will follow those worms as they inch through the living room, under the furniture, into the kitchen and then–

'It's good, yeah,' you answer. 'Easy reading.' You say nothing more than this before going back to burying your stare between the page folds of the novel because you have mastered the art in not overdoing your lies. Your family have started to see when you are bluffing.

*

Your weight is the lowest it's been in six months and you are unhappy. On a Saturday afternoon, now the house is empty, you only sit and stare into the ornaments on the coffee table. There are three Buddha heads there with plastic plants that you think serve the purpose of hair, and then you think what a bastardisation this is. When you run out of ways to feel disappointed for these severed heads and absent bodies, you consider your own: a severed body; an absent head.

The sun is shining – a warm autumnal shine that belongs to September – but you are late October cold. So you make a blanket of your unhappiness; pull it loose around angular shoulders, though you have stopped expecting any comfort from this. ~~Part of you knows better and understands the chill bone sadness is not what you want. But you seldom listen.~~

When your family comes home, they ask what you have been doing all this time. 'Communing with the abyss' is too abstract an answer so instead you wave the same offending paperback; this, your handy prop.

*

27

You cycle Xkm a day on a cross-fit bike. This usually takes you X minutes. But throughout the time you have spent exercising, now, you have managed to whittle this down to X minutes instead. On the days when you do not manage Xkm, or Xkm in X minutes, you feel as though you have failed. Though deep down, you know, it is not you that has failed, it is your body. And of course, your body has failed, because you are not eating.

You think you need to stop exercising for a while. This is a very different statement to, 'I will stop exercising for a while.' The first is what you admit to yourself when the thought of exercising brings you to tears, not because you are in pain but because you are tired. In the same way that sunflowers tire when they are out of season, your stem, while tall, in fact feels *too* tall to support itself and it leaves your head weary and drooping, even though anyone who walks past you at a glance would think you are yellow bright and healthy. The second statement is the lie you tell the people who care about you; the ones who worry that are you exercising/working/generally *doing* too much. You tell them you will stop exercising for a while because it is a conversation closer. It is the easiest way to insert a full stop.

When you started to exercise, months ago, you felt strong. There are times now, or at least recently, when you have also felt strong. But strong does not compare to being able to count your morning calories on your rib cage; child with an abacus happy. So you have to have a serious conversation with yourself about whether the exercise is really worth the need, the basic bodily need, to increase your calorie intake. Most days, you decide that it isn't.

'You're sweating a fair bit this morning,' your relative says when you get home from the gym. Instead of hearing this as an observation, you hear it as a compliment. There is a language barrier somewhere, because you hear: You're sweating a fair bit this morning which probably means you have managed to dehydrate yourself further. Well done for that.

No one would ever say this to you. Your logic brain knows that. But the rest of your brain controls your gear shifts, these days, because you are not intaking enough energy to make your logic brain the dominant voice. That is not the science of the matter but it feels close to what is happening.

'Some days are harder than others, aren't they?' you answer, before leaving the room quickly to shower – or to weigh yourself again. You hope the sound of the shower will cover the sound of you knocking the scales to life, tapping the side of their face and asking if there is anyone there. Sometimes, you imagine your family members wish to do the same to you.

'Everything okay?' your mum asks, later.

You want to answer: No. But you know that it is best to lie. You've started lying to your counsellor, even. You aren't reflecting; you aren't sitting with the sessions. You also aren't doing your homework. What you are doing is lying to the very people who want to help you – this, you're very good at. While your ability to exercise withers, this, lying, you can still do to a gold Olympian standard.

Your mum lets a second or two pass before adding, 'You haven't been yourself since you got back from your trip.' A trip she was nervous of you taking, in case it was less of a break and more of a pilgrimage to starvation.

Instead of answering the actual question, though, you ask, 'How do I not seem okay?' This isn't avoidance, as such. This is you wondering what your tell is.

Nine

Imagine this:

Your body is a studio apartment. You have always been fond of minimalism, which is another way of saying bare, or small. You have decorated the walls, so this is where the eye is drawn when there are visitors. It is a distraction, so they fail to notice that the first thing you did when you moved in was to rip out the kitchen entirely. It was only a counter worktop, with a sink and space for utilities. Though you took a great amount of pleasure in taking this apart with your own hands. Each piece is hidden here, somewhere, though you are unsure of where given the limited space.

Inside this beige landscape – bar the still life portraits of flowers – there is enough space to be comfortable. This is the lie you tell yourself when you begin to unpack feelings and store them in the cracks of the walls and the slimline gaps of the floorboards. You have found that with enough dedication there is always room for these things, that you carry from home to home without knowing why, or understanding what their value is in your life.

There is a two-seater sofa in the living room and a single bed in the lone bedroom. You would have bought an armchair, but you needed to be seen as considerate to guests, and they, too, will need somewhere to sit. The coffee table is glass. The bookshelves are lined with tomes about the body. You have not read any of them, but they help you to portray your desired persona of someone who understands their ~~space~~ place in the world.

When people ask whether you feel that you have nested, you provide noncommittal answers. Your most preferred response is to throw your arms wide and say, This is enough space for me. When you do this, you try to avoid touching the walls either side of you because it highlights that you are the width of the room and this makes you feel self-conscious. When they have gone, you tell yourself that the apartment is okay; enough. You say aloud, I will not be here forever. There is not enough empty air for this to echo back. You do not always know what you mean when you say it.

Ten

You have started to experience dizziness, though you know dizziness is not the word you're looking for when you describe the sensation. There isn't a single verb that describes the tilting of an axis, though, the sudden shift as though the world is now off balance and you, also off balance, are holding onto something that appears fixed. Fixed being a relative term used to describe something that might be weighted down, which is a concept you find unsettling, too. When this begins to happen, you start by ignoring it. You stand up too quickly or rush from one room to another and there the tilt is, but you only freeze for a moment, hang onto the kitchen counter or another convenient landmark within the house, and wait for it to pass.

However, there is one evening when the tilt is so severe that you feel you have shifted to the underbelly of something. Wherever it is, it is dark there, and your vision dims. It comes back seconds later after furious blinks and a quickening of the heartrate, and when it comes, it is a childish kaleidoscope of colours that bleed back together. It is the picture reveal in a 90s gameshow. On the other side of the pixelation, there is the room you started in. You try to think of a caption that would encapsulate this and settle on, There's no place like home.

'You should see a doctor,' your step-parent says.

You haven't told your actual parent what is happening.

Your step-parent says, 'You're not making too much of a thing out of anything. It sounds like your blood pressure is dropping. Are you doing anything, when it happens, that might make your blood pressure drop?'

You consider the night before and the way in which you ran the bath deliberately hot. You think of the prickle of skin when you were submerged in the water; the way your loose stomach became a deflated red balloon. Then, you think of when the bath water became too warm for you to stand it. You think of standing, how you shifted one foot then the other when you settled on the scales and saw you had not dehydrated enough to cause your weight to drop enough.[3] You think of leaving the water to ferment, with Radox dying on its surface, and how when you were a child you might have scooped these bubbles into a plastic saucepan – the yellow one, with blue drawings around its edge, though you can't remember what the drawings were of – and you note the irony, how as a child you enjoyed this practice of making a witch/wizard of yourself and now you are the adult trapped in the mixing pot. You think of turning on the hot tap and running the water through the attached showerhead. You think of hanging your head over the edge of the bath and waiting for the steam to rise. You think of the song that was playing, the one you used to time this process.

You say, 'No, I can't think of anything.'

You see a different doctor to your normal general practitioner. S/He doesn't know about your "eating problems", which is the phrase you use when you are reluctant to give the thing a name. When s/he says, 'And are you taking care of yourself?' You have to ask her/him what s/he means.

'You know, eating, drinking, sleeping, exercising.'

'I exercise regularly,' you say, which is a true answer. 'Sleeping can be patchy but I manage six or seven hours most nights.' You are told this isn't bad, and in your mouth you roll around the lie raised in you, that adults need eight hours of sleep per night. 'I'm in recovery for an eating disorder,' you eventually admit, 'so food can be difficult.'

You are not sure how long it's been since your counsellor left the service and like a chocolate domino your sessions tumbled, too, snapped. He told you the services would still be there if you needed them. To go back, when and if things became hard. You enjoyed the implication that a) things weren't still hard and b) that they mightn't get worse or bad again. At the moment you are doing better than you have been for some time. On *very* good days, you might even

---

3.   Enough is another relative term. You have struggled with this word throughout recovery and relapse. You are not thin enough, you are not sick enough, you are not committed enough to getting better. You want the reader to know you are still struggling with this, and that enough, in recovery, is a word that should be pencil scratched from the dictionary by the angry hand of a child carving something into a school desk.

manage X meals. On difficult days, you manage considerably less. This is recovery.

'How much do you have to drink every day?'

You make a joke about wine but no one in the room laughs.

'I try to have two litres, and I try to make sure it isn't just two litres of caffeine.' This both is and isn't a joke, but this comment, the doctor finds amusing.

'Really, you should be aiming for two litres of water a day. Then things like caffeine, and the rest of anything you drink, all of that goes on top.'

This feels like new information. You had always thought it was two litres of fluid a day. Admittedly, you don't consume this much either. When s/he explains the amount you really need, you realise you are here because of dehydration – or at least, partially so.

The doctor tries to check your oxygen levels and when s/he clips the machine onto your finger s/he says, 'Your hands are really cold, too.'

'I struggle with coldness,' you admit, 'I do try to get warm but it doesn't seem to stick.'

You lock eyes and no one in the room speaks and you are wondering whether they are waiting for you to realise the implications of what you have just said. This isn't new information either, you want to tell them, I am cold because I am not feeding my body with enough energy to stay warm. I'm not stupid, you think of saying. But you don't feel like this would necessarily help.

'You need to be eating and drinking more,' the doctor tells you, after you have told her/him the amount you eat on what you consider to be a good day. You nod, because there are no words big enough to voice your disappointment at this news. The doctor turns back to her/his computer. 'If you eat a little more it will help with the coldness you're experiencing, too.'

Eleven

Imagine this:

Your body is an igloo. It is not spherical, though there are times when you imagine it must be. Instead, it is a catenary curve; it is a distended stomach from refeeding, or from finally drinking the amount of fluid intake you should allow yourself to have. When you lie flat against the earth, you picture your stomach protruding as a perfect mound; structurally adept for keeping your home upright. This ~~food and water~~ shape should reduce the stress placed on your ~~body~~ home as it ages, too. The snow used to shape your igloo is not snow that has rested but rather snow that has been blown. It was caught in the wind once, restless, but this reckless wandering means it has seen enough of the world to be appropriate for building your dome structure. You have heard that a well-built igloo can withstand the pressure of an average size and weight human being standing on top of it, and from past experiences with lovers, friends and people who did not care about you as they should have, you know this to be a truth.

Inside, there are ice crystals hanging from the ceiling that form a dishevelled chandelier. There is a block of freshwater, summer air clear, placed in the wall, and this is where the light gets in. You have started to research affordable insulation because hot water bottles, blankets, and sitting in chilled sunshine no longer keep you comfortable. Though in your mind this should all be quite enough given that igloos, despite reputation, should not be polar chilled but rather steadily warm. You think, too, of the passion that you store within this igloo. Inside, there is a drive and determination that is red in colour; not a dull or salmon red, either, but a brilliant one, Ferrari red, or poppy. Throughout, there are small bundles of projects that you adore and polaroid pictures that detail events you have been to with friends (though, tellingly, there are no pictures of evenings out with friends that involve food, or even drinks anymore, given that you cannot drink on an empty stomach and you have convinced yourself you cannot live happily with a full one). But despite this maroon rose wine, you are chronically frozen.

You wonder whether an air source heat pump might help.

Twelve

You have been thinking a lot of an ex-partner. This feeds the problem ~~and you laugh~~ and only makes you feel worse; though you suspect this is why you do it. You have been thinking, too, of past mistakes; your own, and those belonging to other people. You have sharpened the edges of them to make them into Swiss Army Knives: a corkscrew; a pair of scissors; a lacerated edge. When they are sharp enough to piece flesh – they may have been to start with, you think, but nothing can ever be too sharp – you swallow each one. There are small tears appearing on the inside of your throat, the lining worn ribbon thin. This is your new reason for not eating. Though if you are honest with yourself, it has likely been your reason all along.

Because life has been busy, it has been difficult to maintain the habits that maintain your weight ~~loss~~. Sometimes, it is too late for a long enough bath; sometimes, events take longer to reach their conclusion and habits have to be skipped ~~if you want to keep them hidden~~; sometimes, you are simply too tired. This last one is happening more frequently. You are too tired to deprive yourself though of course, when you do not deprive yourself, this action is weaponised, too. It is emotional warfare where your own finger rests on your own button and you press-press-press like a frustrated middle-aged man at the end of a long work day trying to get a broken television remote to work: press-press-press. Until eventually the remote is flung across the room. You know this is a metaphor, but you aren't sure what it symbolises.

'Shall we go for dinner this weekend?' someone who loves you asks one day, like it's nothing.

You want to say no. But you are trying, hard, to provide answers that anger the thing which you will not give a formal name to. So instead you say, 'That would be lovely.' Now, you can add LIAR to the list of reasons why you should not eat; though of course, that was already there. It sits between PIECE OF SHIT and YOU'RE A SELFISH BITCH and other things you remember people saying to you; other things you have swallowed and nursed like eggs in your belly; eggs that have hatched into ill-feeling. You wonder how much they weigh.

'Where do you want to go?'

You replace 'I don't care' with, 'We'll go wherever you want. Is there something that you fancy?' This reminds you of dieting; the idea of swapping the "unhealthy" option for something greener and easier to digest. 'We could just see how we feel on the day,' you add, knowing this will make you feel worse in many ways. But the guilt you feel for putting your loved ones through this, over and again, is another thing to be weaponised. There is a constant push-pull in your gut now and it causes cramps; though of course, the rumble could be hunger, too.

The day comes when the person who loves you wants to take you out for dinner. Because they love you, they take you to what they know is a safe place; safe in the sense that you have been here before; safe in the sense that you know the menu. But still, you search down the list of meal options and immediately find that you are drawn to the kcals alongside them. You are not interested in any hard or helpful nutritional information. Instead, you fixate for a second or two on the banner across the bottom of the sheet that reads: Based on an adult consumption of Xkcals a day. This number is not an unfamiliar one, but it is still something you cannot trust. You look again at the options – lessened by the fact that you have been vegetarian for over a decade which drastically decreases the well of possibilities listed here – and you opt for, 'Lentil pasta bake.' Because it has the lowest numerical kcals. You wish the government had opted for a more beneficial figure; something that might quantify the amount of guilt you will feel after eating. And while the person who loves you continues to browse the options – their choices are plenty, even though they, too, are vegetarian but unlike you they do not have a hyper-fixation on numbers – you begin to wonder what the abbreviation for guilt would look like if it were printed on a menu. Glt? You wonder, too, then, how this would be quantified.

When the pasta bake – that has Xkcals – is placed in front of you, you stare it down like a Zygiella x-notata: common in the United Kingdom, and ultimately harmless. But it's still disconcerting to see one.

'You're allowed to eat,' your loved one reminds you.

You try to smile as though you are about to tell a joke. 'It's just so much food.'

They reach for your hand. 'But it isn't, sweetheart.'

'It looks like it is.'

'It's a normal portion. I promise.'

Though of course, your perception of normal is distorted. It is the kaleidoscope you peered through as a child. There is a focus point at the centre where, if you try hard enough, you might see something that resembles a concrete shape. But largely, you can only see abstracts. It is all movement and colour. Perceptions of normal are relative, and everything is 'so much' when your normal is someone else's 'not enough'.

You struggle through this dinner. Though everything about the afternoon itself is joyous – that feeling that you periodically permit yourself – apart from the dinner at its core. You tell your loved one that you have had a nice time and when you arrive home you tell other loved ones the same thing because they like to hear it. You find that you are describing everything in Alice in Wonderland terms: 'The dessert was THIS BIG.' You resist the urge to throw your arms open to encompass the room. Though you do list colours and tastes and textures as though you are party to a television cooking series. 'I'd definitely have it again,' you lie, because there is nothing in the world you would definitely have again. Unless your proposal for a Glt figure on menus is taken seriously by your local MP, which you feel is unlikely. But if you could anticipate the guilt, you tell yourself, things would be easier.

The part of your brain still fuelled by logic tries to remind you that alongside every menu the world over it should read: 0Glt. Because food is a basic need in being human – even though you believe you have trained your body free of this bind – and there should never be guilt in allowing yourself that, no matter how bad a person you perceive yourself to be.

While you are regaling your loved ones with this narrative, your parent makes you a cup of tea without asking. You imagine a tag around the handle, something that reads: Drink Me. When you take the cup for your first mouthful, another tag appears. This one reads: ~~Kill Yourself.~~

And this is when you know.

Thirteen

Imagine this:

Your body is a treehouse. Your parents built it for you with inherited materials: which is to say its integrity is not always sound. Their input was shared, with one providing more physical labour than the other; one providing an inherent sense that you will never be enough for anyone, to carry into your adulthood. This has stained the wood in places. Since its conception, the treehouse has developed splinters; there are nails hammered in at awkward angles; in January rain, the roof leaks onto the chessboard of carpet cut-offs. But it is hard to mend these problems. Standing in a skyscraper at the same time as trying to modify it is no easy feat.

The innards, though worn, are open plan and they want [they are wont] to let the light in. There are beanbags that spill polka dots onto the floor; posters of a vampire you thought was especially attractive in season seven of *Buffy the Vampire Slayer*; notes that you and a once friend wrote to each other in a code you no longer remember the hieroglyphics for. It is a treasure chest of formative encounters. In the corner, there is a literal chest that is full of Pringles and chocolate-covered pretzels and crumpets – though there is no toaster – because your remaining parent was told by the people who are trying to help you that having things around that you like (read: might want to eat) will improve your stay here.

You have told them you do not want to live in a treehouse anymore. Which is not the same as saying you do not want to live. And in time you see the distinction between these things. You observe that even as you have grown, this structure has held you; it has always held you. Despite efforts to fingernail pick the paintwork and stress the timber to the point of warping and– Somehow this ~~body~~ treehouse has endured. It has become self-repairing, as though powered by a kind of magic.

Fourteen

Your mental illness becomes a paint-by-numbers experience. You have coloured in the boxes for contacting your GP. You are trying to decide on the colours for liaising with the Mental Health Nurse at your GP's practice and awaiting a referral for the Eating Disorder Team. You are using the thing's name now. When these blocks are eventually coloured, you realise you are borrowing from a spectrum of shades that you have come to associate with the sliding scale of a Body Mass Index Calculator. On the NHS website, you have to scroll past

Understand your BMI result

Why waist size also matters

Children's BMI

Limitations of the BMI

before you arrive at the section marked **Eating disorders**.

You are trying not to read too much about the weight of people with eating disorders. It isn't helpful, you realise. Instead, doing this only creates a tick list of things you are not – which is to say, you are not underweight. It becomes a person specific job application wherein you tick very few of the qualifying boxes and this leads you into a snake and ladders scenario of not feeling sick enough, but still taking tablets every time someone mentions food that you have not planned for. This is a knee-jerk reaction that you tell the Health Worker about the next time you see her.

'There are regular days when I take them,' you explain, 'and then there are special occasions.'

'What counts as a special occasion?'

You shrug. 'A family member's birthday.'

There is a look, then, that speaks of sympathy and understanding, and you want to tell her that you are not deserving of that reaction and that she should save it for someone who is sick enough. You slip down a snake and instead find that you are crying in the Health Worker's office while she explains you are deserving of food as well as help, and you want to call her a liar but it seems rude. You put a foot on the bottom rung of a ladder and say, 'Thank you.' You try to ignore the snakebite sting of this.

After the appointment people will ask how it went and you will say fine. But you will not mention that you weigh less now than you did during your first consultation. It's okay, though, because you are still swimming in the right colour of the pool; your feet can touch the bottom, even if you are treading water with reptiles.

You have to see this same woman periodically while you wait for the next appointment series to arrive. She is a placeholder but a helpful one. You think of sending her a Christmas card and start to wonder what chocolates she likes, or might like, or whether she has more of a savoury tooth. You have written a Christmas list of twenty-four different things that you might buy this woman before realising you are eating by proxy.

'There are foods I miss,' you say when you next see her, even though she has only just asked how you are, and how you have been, between appointments. But somehow, she understands this as an answer.

'Is she helping you?' your parent asks.

'I'm not sure it's her job to.'

'No,' they say, while they are making tea/putting away food shopping/spreading butter onto a crumpet. 'I suppose you're the only one who can do that.'

A snake wraps itself around your ankle and tugs.

'It can't make anything worse, though, seeing her,' you say. You are staring at your laptop screen where colours are swimming in and out of focus and you try to count how many cups of tea you had before this conversation. The Health Worker will ask how your dizzy spells are.

*

A year ago you had a conversation with your sibling ~~where they told you they worried about you being hospitalised~~ where you promised to get better. You do not have a New Year's Resolution, only New Year knowledge: Recovery is hard.

And a year is a very short space of time.

*

There are days when you are hanging your head over a steaming hot bath with the shower head running hot and wishing for the end of this; though you do not always know what you mean when you think that. You share these moments with your shiny new counsellor (the one Santa Claus brought you for Christmas) when they ask if you are still having a red burn bath every night. You do not want to lie to them and you consider this progress.

'What is happening in life at the moment? Away from food?' they ask, and the answers pour from you in a torrent. You are a swimming pool being emptied until all that is left is the bottom of fractured tiles and dirty grout.

'But you can't control any of that.'

Your stomach answers with an animal grunt and you say, 'I know. That's not what food is about.'

There is a long pause before they say, 'It sometimes is, actually.'

This feels like progress, too.

*

'Is the counselling even helping you this time?'

*

You tell your counsellor that your family does not believe in counselling. In that, they make counselling a fairy tale structure of whimsy where the counsellor themselves is both the protagonist and antagonist, and you are the wild princess/prince/person trapped in a tower. Or maybe you are the tower, something that needs to be scaled. Maybe you are the dragon or the witch or the creature under the bridge; maybe you are the dark forest or the rich kingdom or the village that has nothing but beans that are meant to be magic but, in fact, are just ordinary.

'Maybe you are *all* of these things,' your counsellor says. 'Maybe all of us are all of these things. Light and shade, all over, good and bad.' There is dead air on the Zoom call while you process this and you hate that your counsellor can see you thinking. You wonder whether a spider might tumble from your ear, it's been so long since you used this part of your brain – the part that does not run on fury and self-punishment and restriction.

You and your counsellor do not know each other well, yet, though they know more of your innards than anyone else in the world ~~apart from the person who knows and loves you anyway and who you persist in pushing away on the premise that you are unloveable~~. Still, it feels especially intimate when your counsellor clicks the Screen Share option and says, 'I want to show you a poem.'

Wait

Fifteen

Imagine this:

Your body is a guest house stripped from page one-hundred and nine of Rumi's *Selected Poems*. There are frequent visitors; guests you have not prepared for. But you are learning to welcome them. Though there are times when you will need to move the furniture into the napkin square garden to make space for your boarders, you understand, now, this is only to allow them what they need: free territory in which they can deposit their own belongings. On occasion, you feel that you do not have room for these occupants. Their luggage elbows at the corners of your living room; their words clutter the paper where yours were once. You become accusatory, then, that they gift you nothing but sadness when they arrive, and sadness is offended by this. Sadness calls in a motley crew by way of reinforcement. You decide to make them tea.

The tea is chenna coloured according to a Pinterest chart of brown and you make a conversation point of this. Your company is fascinated by the word, words, and the ways in which we are all describing different things meaning the same and vice versa, and the discussion lasts for so long that you are grounded by post office red and parakeet and oxlip. The living room walls are a child's bedroom; one that has been given paint swatches to play with and this collage resembles something like calm, though your parent will likely tell you it looks like a ruin. You will tell them it is a relic.

It soon becomes clear that your tenants have good intentions even if they are bastards to live with. They do not help you to piece back together the rooms as they were before they arrived. But you come to appreciate this is part of the worth in their visit. You are learning this re-piecing as an act of kindness; a bloodied and bruising and messy act, but still. There are times, you see now, when these major renovations – breaking down the chemical bonds ~~of neurotransmitters~~ of paint and finding easier shades to live with – is the softest thing you can do for your ~~body~~ home. Even though there will always be more visitors; there will always be restoration, too.

Acknowledgements

YOUR UNREST IS A HOUSE LAID OUT